PRINCESS PULVERIZER

yo-ho, yo . . . NO!

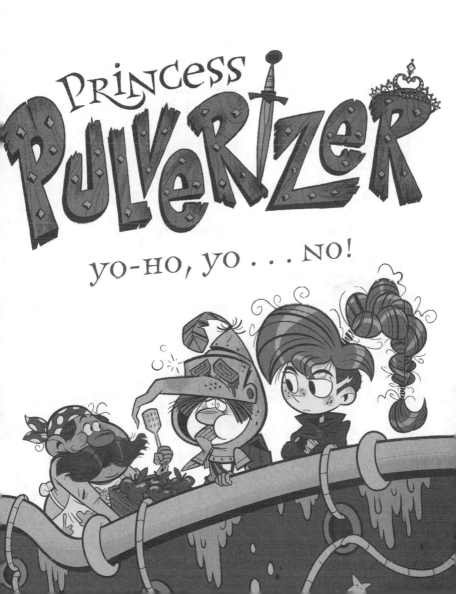

PENGUIN WORKSHOP
An Imprint of Penguin Random House LLC, New York

Text copyright © 2020 by Nancy Krulik. Illustrations and logo copyright © 2020 by
Penguin Random House LLC. All rights reserved. Published by Penguin Workshop,
an imprint of Penguin Random House LLC, New York. PENGUIN and PENGUIN
WORKSHOP are trademarks of Penguin Books Ltd, and the W colophon is a
registered trademark of Penguin Random House LLC. Printed in the USA.

Visit us online at www.penguinrandomhouse.com.

Art colored by Joven Paul

Library of Congress Control Number: 2019033539

ISBN 9781524791599 (pbk)   10 9 8 7 6 5 4 3 2 1
ISBN 9781524791605 (hc)   10 9 8 7 6 5 4 3 2 1

NANCY KRULIK

PRINCESS PULVERIZER

YO-HO, YO . . . NO!

art by Ian McGinty
based on original character designs by
Ben Balistreri

Penguin Workshop

For teachers, who open the minds and hearts
of the next generation—NK

To Samantha, a princess and pulverizer—IM

CHAPTER 1

"I'm boiling in here," Lucas said, lifting his visor higher over his head. "It's not easy wearing armor in hot weather."

Princess Pulverizer frowned. Lucas had no right to complain. She'd give anything to be wearing armor in this—or any— weather. All Princess Pulverizer had ever wanted to be was a knight in shining armor.

Not that Lucas's armor was particularly shining. It was more like *rusting*. But still . . .

"It's definitely warm out," Dribble the dragon said. "Even hotter than my flame!"

Dribble was exaggerating, of course. But it *was* a hot day. And to make things worse, there was a terrible stink in the air. Where was that coming from, anyway?

The princess sniffed under her armpits. Yikes! The stink was coming from *her*. Quickly she lowered her arms to hide the stains forming under her armpits.

Caw. Caw. Caw.

Princess Pulverizer looked up to see three gray-and-white birds fly by. "How about we find a nice sea breeze?" she suggested.

Dribble looked around. "I don't see any

water. Just dirt and grass."

"There must be a beach over those hills," Princess Pulverizer said, pointing up at the birds. "Where there are seagulls, there's usually a sea."

"I could go for a swim in the ocean," Dribble said.

"Not me," Lucas said. "I'm a terrible swimmer. But I *would* like to go somewhere cooler."

"Then it's settled," Princess Pulverizer said. "Follow those birds!"

◆ ◆ ◆ ◆ ◆

"We'll battle storms, hoist the sails,
and pray we stay afloat.
For we are sailors all our lives
and loyal to this boat."

When she and her friends reached the beach, Princess Pulverizer spotted a ship and some sailors. They were cleaning their ship and checking the sails for rips and tears. As they worked, they sang joyfully.

*"Sail, sail, sail the ship.
To where, we do not know.
A sailor's life is in the hands
of winds that always blow."*

"Hey! I know that song," Princess Pulverizer said excitedly. "The sailors in Empiria sing it all the time." She began to sing along. *Loudly.* "Sail, sail, sail the ship . . ."

The sailors stopped singing and stared.

Lucas frowned.

Dribble shook his head.

"What?" Princess Pulverizer demanded.

"Well . . . it's just that . . . I mean, it's not your fault . . . ," Lucas stammered.

"What my little buddy is trying to say is, you can't sing," Dribble told her finally.

Princess Pulverizer scowled. "What do you mean I can't sing?"

"I mean you're off-key, out of tune, and have no rhythm," Dribble replied.

"But you have other talents," Lucas assured her.

"Lots of them," Dribble agreed. "You do quite well at fencing, for instance."

"And climbing trees," Lucas continued.

"You think fast and have clever ideas," Dribble added.

Princess Pulverizer stopped scowling. Those *were* important talents. Especially for someone who wanted to join the Knights of the Skround Table someday. Which was the very reason Princess Pulverizer was out here in the broiling sun in the first place. She was on a Quest of Kindness, searching for a good deed to do.

Like a real knight.

When Princess Pulverizer had first asked her father, King Alexander, if she could go to Knight School, he'd flat out told her no.

But she hadn't given up. She'd begged. Pleaded. And even given her father her special face: the one where she cocked her head to the side and crossed her eyes. That *never* failed to help the princess get her way.

And sure enough, the princess was able to convince King Alexander to let her go to Knight School—exactly as she'd expected.

Just not right away.

Which she had *not* expected.

King Alexander would only let Princess Pulverizer enter Knight School after she went on a Quest of Kindness and completed eight good deeds.

Princess Pulverizer had now been on her Quest of Kindness for what seemed a very long time. With the help of her new friends, Lucas and Dribble, she'd done *a lot* of good deeds.

Like outwitting a wily wizard.

Winning out over a wicked witch.

And uniting a family of unicorns.

In all, the three friends had completed seven good deeds. Along the way, the princess had learned all about teamwork, selflessness, and kindness.

Now Princess Pulverizer was excited to find an eighth good deed to do—the last on her Quest of Kindness. Knight School was so close she could smell it.

But she could also smell herself. And she was stinky. *Yuck.*

The princess reached into her knapsack and pulled out her hand mirror. Sure enough, her face was filthy, and her hair was matted and greasy.

As Princess Pulverizer stared at her reflection, the image changed. She no longer saw herself as she was now. Rather, she saw herself with a sword drawn, and her legs poised to advance on an unseen enemy.

The mirror was showing Princess Pulverizer what the future held. Which was no surprise, because that was what the magic mirror always did.

〈13〉

Unfortunately, the magic mirror didn't tell the princess where or when she would be in a sword fight. Or whom she would be fighting.

Could this be a practice fight, taking place in Knight School? She certainly hoped so.

But in order to make that happen, the princess had to find one more person to help so she could complete her quest for good deeds. There just didn't seem to be anyone around but those sailors. And they didn't appear to be in need of any assistance.

At one time, the princess would have been pushing her friends to move on so they could find another good deed to do right away. But Princess Pulverizer was trying hard to learn patience.

So perhaps the quest could wait while they cooled off in the ocean.

"I'm going in the water," she told her friends. "Who's with me?"

"In a minute," Dribble said, scratching his shoulder. "I've got this itch on my back that I can't reach."

"I got you." Lucas began scratching Dribble's scaly green back.

"Thanks, little buddy," Dribble said.

"Hey," Lucas said as he scratched. "Your wings are getting bigger!"

"You really think so?" Dribble asked excitedly.

"Definitely," Lucas said. "Maybe that's why you're so itchy. Do dragon wings itch when they grow?"

"I don't know," Dribble replied. "I can't wait to have my grown-up wings, though.

Then I'll finally be able to fly."

Princess Pulverizer yanked off her boots and started toward the water's edge. But before she could dip even a toe into the ocean, she heard more singing.

This time, though, the song wasn't familiar.

It wasn't joyful.

And it wasn't coming from the sailors.

It was a woman's voice. And it was beautiful.

Also very, *very* sad.

*"Set me free
to swim in the sea.
To flutter and float
away from this boat."*

"Do you hear that?" Princess Pulverizer

asked Lucas and Dribble.

Lucas and Dribble stood quiet for a moment.

"Set me free
to swim in the sea."

"It's a cry for help," Princess Pulverizer said, pulling her boots back on.

"I guess we're not going for a swim," Dribble told Lucas.

"We'll swim after we've freed whoever's singing," Princess Pulverizer assured her pals. "Right now, we have a good deed to do!"

CHAPTER 2

"Someone is trapped in a fishing net!"
Dribble exclaimed as the three friends
arrived at a small cove. There, they found
the singer of the sad song, struggling
to free herself from a prison of knotted
ropes floating on the water's surface, not
far from land. The ropes appeared to be
attached to the nearby ship.

"Poor woman," Lucas added.

"That's no woman," Princess Pulverizer told her friends.

"Sure it is," Lucas insisted. "Look at her face. And her hair. And her . . ."

"*Tail*," Princess Pulverizer finished his sentence. "She's a mermaid."

"A *real* mermaid?" Lucas asked in amazement.

"*Duh.* Of course I'm real," the mermaid bellowed in an angry, tough voice. "Whoever heard of a *fake* mermaid? Sheesh." She began combing her hair with a pearl-covered comb.

"I'm sorry," Lucas said. He looked at her curiously. "You don't *talk* like a mermaid."

"What's a mermaid s'posed to talk like?" the mermaid demanded.

"I don't know," Lucas admitted. "I've never met a mermaid before."

"Yeah, well, I never met a kid in a rusted tin can before," the mermaid replied.

"It's not a tin can." Lucas sounded hurt.

"That's his armor," Dribble explained. "It's just old."

"And small," Lucas said. "I think it shrank in the last rainstorm."

"Armor doesn't shrink," Dribble told him. "You've grown. Soon I won't even be able to call you *little* buddy."

The mermaid stared at Dribble for a long moment. "Yo, dude," she said. "Are you a dragon?"

"He is. But you don't have to worry about him," Princess Pulverizer replied. "He uses his fire to make grilled cheese."

"Make *what*?" the mermaid asked.

"You've never heard of grilled cheese?" The princess was surprised. "It's cheese melted onto toasted bread."

"It's not like we eat a lot of bread underwater, you know," the mermaid snapped back. "It gets kinda soggy."

Well, that made sense.

Dribble nodded. "You've never

had grilled cheese?" he said. "I feel bad for you."

The mermaid shook the ropes that were holding her captive. "*That's* why you feel bad for me? Seriously?" she said, rolling her eyes.

Dribble didn't answer.

"The name's Meri, by the way," she continued.

"I'm Princess Pulverizer," the princess introduced herself. "This is Dribble, and that's Lucas."

"Pleased to meetcha," Meri said. "Sorry if I'm staring. I don't get to see too many land folks up close. We're s'posed ta stay away from ya. Now I know why." She pulled angrily at the ropes tied all around her. "When I get outta here, I'll never swim near a ship again, I swear!"

‹23›

"How did you get tangled up in that net?" Princess Pulverizer asked her.

"Pirates," Meri explained, pointing toward the side of the large ship anchored in the cove. "This net is tied to the side of their ship." She splashed around angrily.

Princess Pulverizer looked up. She'd been so focused on Meri, she hadn't noticed the droopy black-and-white flag with the skull on it hanging from a pole way up on the ship's deck. At least the princess *thought* it was a skull. There were so many holes in the flag, it was hard to tell. Also the paint was peeling, the wood was warped, and the sails were sagging. It was the saddest pirate ship Princess Pulverizer had ever seen.

It was also the *only* pirate ship Princess Pulverizer had ever seen.

The princess was so excited, she could barely contain herself. She was standing barely three feet away from an actual pirate ship!

"Why would pirates want to capture you?" Dribble asked.

"Captain Bobbie thinks I know where to find sunken treasure," Meri said. "Pirates *love* treasure. They won't set me free until I take 'em to it."

"At least they figured out a way to keep you in the water," Lucas suggested.

"Yeah, well, they do kinda need me alive if they want me to talk," Meri barked back. "Sheesh."

Ordinarily, Princess Pulverizer might have leaped to Lucas's defense. After all, he was only trying to find some sort of bright side to Meri's situation. But truthfully, Princess Pulverizer wasn't really listening anymore. Her mind was elsewhere.

Sunken treasure! Pirates! A mermaid! What an adventure this was turning out to be.

"*Do* you know where the sunken treasure is?" Princess Pulverizer asked excitedly.

Dribble shot her a look.

Oops. That hadn't been very knightly. "I'm sorry," she quickly added. "I meant, if you know where it is, why don't you just tell them?"

"I don't want 'em thinkin' they can go around capturin' mermaids to find treasure," Meri explained.

Princess Pulverizer nodded. "Very wise," she said as she held her sword at the ready.

"Hey!" Meri exclaimed in fear.

"Don't worry, I'm just using this to cut you free," Princess Pulverizer told the mermaid.

"A kid like you knows her way around a sword?" Meri sounded surprised.

"I'm quite skilled." The princess waved her weapon dramatically in the air. "I used this very sword to defeat a famous knight. He'd kidnapped my friends and others. No one else was able to beat him. Whole armies had tried. But during our . . ."

"Oh brother," Dribble groaned behind the princess's back.

"She could go on awhile," Lucas warned Meri.

"I will use this same sword to free you," the princess continued. "*Easy peasy*. In three—no, make it *two*—strokes, I'll release you. And then . . ."

Suddenly, Princess Pulverizer felt something sharp poking her in the back. "What the . . . ," she began.

Meri gasped.

"Yikes!" Lucas shouted.

"Uh-oh!" Dribble exclaimed.

"Avast, landlubber!" said a fourth, unfamiliar voice. "Make another move and I'll keelhaul ye."

Huh?

Princess Pulverizer had no idea what that meant. But she knew it wasn't good.

CHAPTER 3

"I don't feel so well," Lucas groaned.

Lucas's face was almost as green as Dribble's. Princess Pulverizer thought he might puke any minute.

"That makes good sense, matey," one of the pirates told Lucas. "Yer on *The Seasick Soaker*. Nothing can steady this ship."

Princess Pulverizer turned her feet out and bent her knees as she struggled to stand while the boat rocked back and forth beneath her.

"The Seasick Soaker," Dribble repeated. "From the smell of this ship, it's got the right name. I think a lot of people have thrown up on this deck."

The dragon held a beautifully embroidered handkerchief to his nose. Its fabric had magical powers—when you held it to your nose, you could smell things that were far away. "Aahhh . . . ," Dribble said. "That's better. Now I smell fresh-baked bread. Must be from a bakery in a nearby town."

Princess Pulverizer wished she had a magic handkerchief as well. The stench on the boat was really foul.

On the bright side, at least no one aboard would notice how badly she stank at the moment. She still hadn't had a chance to rinse off.

"*Argh!* Let me look at these prisoners!" Suddenly, a woman with long red hair and deep green eyes stomped onto the deck. She was wearing brown pants tucked into black leather boots. She wore a red bandanna tied over her head. "Did ye drag all three aboard?"

"Aye, Cap'n Bobbie," a pirate who had been guarding Princess Pulverizer and her friends replied.

Princess Pulverizer looked at Cap'n Bobbie with surprise. She hadn't expected a woman to captain a pirate ship.

Then again, she was pretty sure some people wouldn't expect a princess to become a knight. Which Princess Pulverizer most definitely would be one day.

As soon as she got off this boat.

But that wasn't going to be easy. Already Cap'n Bobbie was making plans to put her new prisoners to work.

"It would be such a waste to just throw the three of ye in the brig," the captain mused. "Yer strong enough to work as part of me crew. Especially this dragon. He'll come in handy. I love burning villages."

"But I don't . . . ," Dribble began.

Cap'n Bobbie glared at him.

Dribble shut his mouth.

"We didn't volunteer to be part of your crew," Princess Pulverizer insisted.

"Have ye met me argument-ender?" Cap'n Bobbie held her sharp, curved sword close to Princess Pulverizer's throat. "Don't challenge me."

Princess Pulverizer gulped.

"I'd be quiet if I were ye," one of the pirates whispered to Princess Pulverizer as Cap'n Bobbie walked away. "She learned how to be mean from her father. And he was fierce."

"Her father allowed her to become a pirate?" Princess Pulverizer asked.

"Only after she sailed the seven seas and completed eight bad deeds," the pirate responded.

Eight deeds. That sounds familiar.

"If she's captain now, where'd her father go?" Lucas wondered.

"Over there." The pirate pointed to the stern of the ship.

"That guy mopping the deck?" Dribble asked.

"Aye. Old Cap'n Stanley," the pirate replied. "We just call him Stinky Stanley now. Cap'n Bobbie put him to work as a deck swabber. Nastiest job on the ship, considering what happens whenever one of us gets seasick."

"Her own father?" Princess Pulverizer was shocked.

"I told ye she was mean," the pirate told her.

◆ ◆ ◆ ◆ ◆

"I don't think we're ever getting out of here," Lucas said as the sun set a few hours later.

The princess and her friends were huddled together in a corner of the ship far from any nosy pirates who might want to listen in on their conversation. There was no one around other than a few noisy seagulls.

That was okay. Seagulls told no tales.

"I can't believe we're stuck on this ship," Dribble grumbled. "What a mess."

"It's not a mess at all," Princess Pulverizer argued. "We're in the best place possible to free Meri. That's what we're trying to do, right?"

"Of course," Lucas agreed. "But how do you figure being on *The Seasick Soaker* will help her?"

"Cap'n Bobbie is sure to set sail soon," Princess Pulverizer explained. "If we were still on land, the ship would sail away with Meri in tow. We'd never be able to reach her. But being on board, we're close enough to cut her free."

"If you'd just stopped bragging long enough to cut her free while we were on land, she would *be* free, and so would we," Dribble pointed out. "But noooooo. You had to make that whole speech."

Princess Pulverizer opened her mouth . . . and shut it again. There was no point in arguing. Dribble was right.

But there was also no going back in time. They were here now. And they needed a plan—which, luckily, Princess Pulverizer had already devised.

"What we need to do is escape and get close enough to Meri to cut her loose," the princess began.

"Obviously," Dribble said. "We all agree on that. The question is, *how* do we escape? It's not like we can just walk down the gangplank. The pirates guard that all the time."

The princess had already figured that out. "I saw a porthole we can use. We'll sneak down to it in the middle of the night, break the glass, and crawl through."

"But the pirate bunks are on the same side of the ship as the porthole," Lucas pointed out. "Surely they will hear us."

"I was thinking about the porthole on the other side of the ship. There's nothing there but storage," Princess Pulverizer said. "It's where Cap'n Bobbie locked up the magic sword, my arrow, and the big mace. I'm going to need that sword to free Meri. Dribble, you're strong enough to break the lock, right?"

"I can try," Dribble said.

"That porthole isn't on the same side of the ship as Meri's net," Lucas pointed out. "There's nothing out the window but water."

"Not a problem," Princess Pulverizer replied. "We'll swim around the boat to the beach side of the cove. Then I'll cut Meri loose. It's the perfect plan."

"For you, maybe," Lucas said. "But Dribble's too big to fit through a porthole, and I don't swim all that well."

Princess Pulverizer thought about that.

"How about I sneak out, swim to Meri, and free her," Princess Pulverizer suggested. "Then I'll create a distraction so big it gets the attention of every pirate on the ship. You two can then walk down the gangplank unnoticed."

"What kind of distraction?" Lucas asked.

"I'll think of something," the princess assured him. "Don't I always?"

"It's worth a try." Dribble scratched at his back. "I've got to get off this ship. My back's itchier than ever. I might have lice."

"It's settled," Princess Pulverizer said. "We'll meet near the porthole after everyone is asleep, and put my—I mean *our*—plan in motion!"

◆ ◇ ◆ ◇ ◆

"This place is nasty," Dribble complained later that night as the three heroes snuck down into the belly of the boat. "Did you see the size of that rat?"

"That wasn't a rat," Lucas said. "It was a water bug. *That's* a rat." He pointed to a huge rodent—one almost the size of a cocker spaniel.

"Do you think anyone followed us?" Dribble asked the others.

"Nope," Princess Pulverizer said. "You had the ruby ring on your tail, and its magic let you walk in complete silence. With us riding on your back, we made no noise at all."

Whoosh! Another huge water bug whizzed by.

"Ugh! That one touched my foot," Lucas said. "Let's get out of here."

"Give me a minute," Dribble said. He reached over and pulled on the metal lock that was protecting the locker where their swords, arrow, and mace were being stored.

Bam! The lock popped open.

Princess Pulverizer held out her arms. "Give me that mace. If I swing it hard enough, it will break the glass."

"STOP RIGHT THERE!"

Before Princess Pulverizer could take a single swing, Cap'n Bobbie came racing down the stairs, with three pirates in tow. Her dark gray parrot was perched on her shoulder.

"Did ye really think ye could escape through the porthole?" the captain demanded. "And what kind of distraction do ye think would keep me from noticing a green dragon running down the gangplank?"

"How did you know . . . ?" Dribble began.

"*Rawk*. Distraction," Cap'n Bobbie's parrot squawked. "*Rawk*. Gangplank."

"The parrot! He was hiding in that flock of seagulls!" Princess Pulverizer exclaimed.

"Parry is me top spy," Cap'n Bobbie said.

"*Parry the parrot?*" Dribble repeated. "That's the best name you could come up with?"

Cap'n Bobbie glared at him. "Ye have a problem with it?" she demanded.

"Um . . . nope." Dribble scratched at his back nervously.

"I'll be keeping an even more keen eye on ye three landlubbers," Cap'n Bobbie declared. "Forget about freeing that mermaid—or escaping. You're on *The Seasick Soaker* for life. However long— *or short*—that may be."

CHAPTER 4

"Stroke!" Princess Pulverizer called out,
directing the crew of pirates as
they pulled on their oars.
"Stroke!"

Truthfully, the princess didn't see any point in all this rowing. *The Seasick Soaker* was still anchored in the cove. It wasn't going anywhere, no matter how hard these men pulled.

But Cap'n Bobbie had put the princess in charge of the rowers. And she'd told her to keep them rowing. So row they did. Boy, was Cap'n Bobbie mean.

Princess Pulverizer couldn't imagine why Cap'n Bobbie had put her in charge of anything. Any one of the rowers could do it. And they'd all been around much longer than she had.

Of course, there would have been plenty of fighting among them if she picked one of them to boss the others around. So maybe this was a good move on the captain's part.

If she was being honest, Princess Pulverizer liked being in charge of something—even if it was just a rowing crew that wasn't going anywhere.

"Sit still, Wiggle-Butt Willy," one of the rowers called out. "You're rocking the bench back and forth."

"Can't help it, Three-Toed Tommy. Me legs itch," Wiggle-Butt Willy replied.

"At least ye *have* two legs," another pirate called to him. "An alligator got one of mine."

"You tell him, Peg-Leg Pete!" Tommy agreed. "That same gator ate two of me toes for dessert—right after he made a dinner out of yer leg."

"He was one hungry gator," Pete agreed.

Princess Pulverizer frowned. The pirates were so busy talking, they had stopped rowing. If Cap'n Bobbie saw this . . .

"STROKE!" Princess Pulverizer shouted, trying to sound in charge.

The pirates quieted down immediately and began rowing again.

Wow. Princess Pulverizer was pretty good at this boss thing, if she did say so herself.

Which she wouldn't. Because bragging wasn't knightly.

It was also what had gotten her into this mess in the first place. Somehow, she had to find a way to free Meri and get off this boat, along with Dribble and Lucas.

But as of yet, she hadn't come up with a new idea of how to do that. So until she did—

"Stroke!" Princess Pulverizer called out. "Stroke!"

◆ ◆ ◆ ◆ ◆

"Give me one of them cheese sandwiches,"
Three-Toed Tommy said as Princess
Pulverizer and the rowing crew entered
the galley for their short lunch break.

Dribble plopped a grilled cheddar on
rye on a chipped plate and handed it to
Tommy.

"Me too," Wiggle-Butt Willy said. "They look better than our usual slop."

A chubby pirate with a big red face bounded out of the kitchen. "What did you say?" he bellowed.

"Sorry, Cookie," Willy told him. "But them sandwiches look tastier than your grub."

"Smell better, too," Stinky Stanley pointed out.

"I'm surprised ye can smell anything, the way ye stink," Cookie told Stanley.

Princess Pulverizer frowned. She knew

she smelled pretty bad, too. She still hadn't had a chance to wash up like she'd planned. But at least she wasn't as stinky as Stanley. Next to him, she smelled like roses.

"So you're finally a chef," she told Dribble.

"Yeah," Dribble agreed. "Cap'n Bobbie figured my flames were cheaper than firewood for cooking."

"The pirates really like your sandwiches," Princess Pulverizer said. "It's kind of a dream come true."

Dribble shook his head. "More like a nightmare. I don't want to cook for *them*."

"What am I supposed to do with all this slop?" Cookie demanded of the pirates.

"Eat it yourself," Three-Toed Tommy said. "Or feed it to the dragon."

"Yeah, let him eat it," Stinky Stanley agreed.

"Go ahead, dragon." Cookie held up a big bowl of steaming gray slop. "Take a spoonful."

"No, thanks," Dribble said.

"Ye don't have a choice!" Cookie bellowed. "I'm the boss in the galley. And I say yer gonna eat it."

Dribble dipped a spoon into the slop, then took a taste.

"This is awful."

"What did ye say?" Cookie growled.

"It's . . . *um* . . . awfully *good*," Dribble corrected himself.

"Aye," Cookie replied. "So get eatin'.

There's lots of slop."

Dribble took another spoonful. He frowned as the pasty stuff slid down his throat and . . .

Dribble let out a belch so powerful, it lifted him right up in the air. Where he stayed for several seconds before . . .

Thud. He landed on his bottom. Hard.

"That was some burp!" Princess Pulverizer exclaimed. "It was like you were flying. How'd you do that?"

"I have no idea," Dribble admitted.

"Yer gonna be sorry, dragon!" Cookie shouted angrily. He was covered in slop. The wind from Dribble's belch had splashed it all over him.

"Like I said, that was some burp." Princess Pulverizer laughed.

◆ ◆ ◆ ◆ ◆

"Pirates take whate'er we want.
We never ask permission.
Gettin' rich from what ye got
is our only mission.
I know ye got some silver

and doubloons all made of gold.
Don't go lookin' for yer gemstones
'cause they've all been stoled."

Princess Pulverizer shook her head. *Stoled* wasn't even a word.

Still, it felt good to be up on deck in the fresh air. Cap'n Bobbie had given the rowers a break—but only so they could plug a big hole in the bow of *The Seasick Soaker*. Which was a good thing. A hole in a boat could give a kid a real *sinking* feeling.

Princess Pulverizer smiled slightly as she noticed Lucas mopping the deck. On a ship full of vicious pirates, it was nice to spot a friend.

Lucas didn't smile back. He wasn't happy to be working with Stinky Stanley.

"Yer gettin' to be a good deck swabber," Stanley told Lucas. "Soon you'll fer sure be a real freebooter."

"A real what?" Lucas asked.

"Freebooter," Stanley repeated. "A pirate."

Lucas looked like he might cry. But before he could let out a single sob, Peg-Leg Pete called out to him, "Hey, kid, we need someone to climb up the mast and check the spars. Get climbin'."

"Check the what?" Lucas asked.

"The spars," Pete repeated. "Those poles up there."

"I—I don't like heights," Lucas admitted.

"Either ye climb, or ye walk the plank," Pete replied. "I hear the sharks are hungry today."

Princess Pulverizer opened her mouth to volunteer to climb the mast for Lucas. But before she could say a word, Lucas rubbed the lion charm around his neck—

the one with the magical power to make its wearer brave.

He put down his mop and began to climb the mast.

The princess was amazed. Lucas was going really high up, but he didn't seem to be crying even a bit. That magic pendant sure was something!

"Pretty good," Peg-Leg Pete called up to him. "Every pirate needs a nickname. I think yers should be Brave Buccaneer."

Even from down on the deck, Princess Pulverizer could see Lucas smiling. Brave Buccaneer was a much better nickname than Lucas the Lily-Livered. It would be something for him to tell the boys in Knight School.

If he ever went back to Knight School.

Sadly, the longer they stayed on *The Seasick Soaker*, the bigger that *if* seemed to become.

CHAPTER 5

"Are ye sure?" Cap'n Bobbie bellowed at Meri.

Princess Pulverizer looked down at the net that was tied to the side of the ship. It had only been a few days, but Meri already looked different from when they first met. The mermaid seemed too tired to splash at all. Her once-shiny hair was now dull. The pearl comb hung limply from the damp strands.

Not being able to swim freely was
taking its toll on her.

"Yeah, I'm sure." Meri sighed. "The
sunken treasure is off the shore of the tiny
island to the west."

Cap'n Bobbie smiled triumphantly. "It
was wise of ye to tell me, mermaid."

"Ya remember the deal we made, don'tcha?" Meri asked, her voice weak yet still gruff. "Ya gonna free me?"

"I always keep me word," Cap'n Bobbie stated.

Princess Pulverizer couldn't believe her ears. It sounded like Meri had given up the location of the treasure. And like Cap'n Bobbie was going to set her free.

Princess Pulverizer frowned. One of them was lying. But which one? With her sword of truth locked up, it was impossible to tell.

"Prepare to set sail at sunset!" Cap'n Bobbie shouted to the crew.

"What the . . . !" Meri began, mustering enough energy to confront the captain. "Ya said you'd free me."

"I will," Cap'n Bobbie answered. "As

soon as I have me hands on that treasure."

Princess Pulverizer sighed. Meri should have seen that coming. Cap'n Bobbie was no fool.

◊　◊　◊　◊　◊

"Whoa!" Lucas shouted as *The Seasick Soaker* sailed out of the cove into the ocean at sunset. "The ship sure is rocking."

"I don't understand why," Dribble said. "The water is smooth. Not a wave in sight."

"Do you think this ship is safe to sail?" Lucas asked Princess Pulverizer.

The princess didn't answer. She was too busy staring at the shore as it grew more and more distant. This was bad. And not just for Meri.

When King Alexander had sent Princess Pulverizer off on her Quest of Kindness, he had clearly instructed, "You may only go as far as the mountains to the east and the river to the west. You may travel as far as the ocean to the south, and to the canyon to the north."

But now Princess Pulverizer was heading *into* the ocean. King Alexander would not be happy she'd defied him.

He might even use this as a reason not to let her go to Knight School! Her father could get really angry if someone didn't follow his orders.

Princess Pulverizer couldn't let that happen.

She could jump overboard and swim to shore now, before the ship got any farther. She was a strong swimmer. She would make it back to land.

But that would mean leaving Dribble and Lucas behind. They weren't nearly as strong swimmers as she was. Without her, they would probably spend the rest of their days on *The Seasick Soaker*. And there was no telling what Cap'n Bobbie might do to her friends when she discovered Princess Pulverizer had gone missing.

The princess couldn't leave Meri behind, either. Being a prisoner was terrible for her. The mermaid was getting weaker and weaker by the hour. Princess Pulverizer doubted Cap'n Bobbie was the kind of person to keep her word. Without help, Meri might never be free.

Still, it was never wise to disobey her father . . .

No! Princess Pulverizer would *not* leave them all behind. She had to stay, for their sakes. She'd made her decision. And it was the most knightly decision Princess Pulverizer had ever made.

Which was really sad. Because as the land began to disappear from view, Princess Pulverizer had a terrible feeling that her dreams of going to Knight School were disappearing, too.

Chapter 6

"Ye better get up and go down to the mess, or ye won't get any grub."

Princess Pulverizer opened one eye. Her quarters were still pretty dark, but she could tell there was someone standing over her bed. Someone who looked a lot like Lucas.

But he sure didn't *sound* like Lucas.

"What did you say?" Princess Pulverizer asked.

"I said you better wake up and go to the galley or there won't be any breakfast left for you," Lucas replied.

"That's not what you said the first time," Princess Pulverizer told him. "You sounded more pirate-y."

Lucas frowned. "You don't think I'm turning into one of *them*, do you?"

"Of course not." Princess Pulverizer tried to sound reassuring. But the truth was, Lucas was acting more and more like the crew of *The Seasick Soaker*. They all were.

The Seasick Soaker had been sailing for three days already. Each day on the water took Princess Pulverizer farther and farther away from Empiria.

Away from her father.

Away from her dream of becoming a knight.

But Princess Pulverizer wasn't giving up. She *was* going to free Meri, get home, and convince her father that she had done the right thing by staying aboard *The Seasick Soaker*.

She would come up with a plan sooner or later. She always did.

Grumble. Rumble.

That was Princess Pulverizer's stomach. It was empty. And the princess knew from experience that she couldn't think on an empty stomach.

"What's Dribble making this morning?" she asked Lucas.

"Baked brie and strawberry jam on toast," he replied.

The princess leaped to her feet. "That's one of his best breakfasts!" she exclaimed. "What are we doing standing around here talking? Let's get to the mess before it's all gone!"

◆ ◆ ◆ ◆ ◆

"Gimme another one of yer sandwiches, dragon," Three-Toed Tommy called to Dribble. "They're delicious."

"Gimme another, too," Peg-Leg Pete said.

As Dribble cooked up two more baked

brie and strawberry jam on white toast
sandwiches, Princess Pulverizer couldn't
help but notice how angry Cookie looked.
The pirate was standing there with a
big tub of gruel that no one wanted.
His face was so red, he nearly matched
the strawberry jam inside Dribble's
sandwiches.

"At least the grub's good," Wiggle-Butt
Willy said. "Not much else to make us
happy these days. Cap'n Bobbie's in a foul
mood."

"Sure is," Stinky Stanley agreed. "Me own daughter, and she threatened to skewer me gizzard if I looked her in the eye."

"I hope Cap'n Bobbie spots that island quick," Three-Toed Tommy said. "If she doesn't get her hands on that sunken treasure, she's liable to scuttle the whole crew." He drew his finger across his neck.

"I can hear her now." Peg-Leg Pete put his hands on his hips and glared at them all the way Cap'n Bobbie so often did. "If ye don't do what I say, I'll keelhaul the lot of ye!"

The other pirates chuckled.

Just then, Cap'n Bobbie stormed angrily into the galley.

"WHAT'S SO FUNNY?"

Pete gulped and quickly sat down beside

the other pirates. "Nuthin', Cap'n."

"That's what I thought," Cap'n Bobbie growled. She turned to Cookie. "What's the grub today?" she asked.

"Fresh porridge," he replied proudly. "I'll get ye a bowl."

Cap'n Bobbie looked around at her crew. "No, I'll have what me men are eatin'. That looks good."

Cookie looked so boiling mad, Princess Pulverizer thought steam might burst out of his ears.

"Cap'n, these sandwiches are made with str . . . ," Stinky Stanley began. But before he could finish his sentence, Cookie shoved a heaping spoonful of porridge in his mouth. With that sticky stuff between his teeth, Stanley couldn't say a word.

Dribble placed a sandwich in front

of Cap'n Bobbie. "Hope you like it, Captain," he said.

"I *better*." Cap'n Bobbie took a bite. "Not bad," she said, taking another big mouthful.

"Thank you," Dribble replied. "Baked brie and strawberry jam is my specialty."

Phtooey! Cap'n Bobbie spat the half-chewed second bite onto the floor.

"STRAWBERRY JAM?" she shouted. "I'm allergic to strawberries. Are ye trying to kill me, dragon?"

Dribble gulped. "No," he insisted. "I didn't know. No one told me."

Princess Pulverizer looked at Cookie. He was biting his lip, trying not to laugh.

"What was strawberry jam doing on me ship, anyway?" the captain demanded.

"I didn't bring it on board," Cookie contended. "The prisoners did. It was in one of their sacks."

"I'm sorry," Dribble said.

But Cap'n Bobbie was too busy scratching the big red welts that had popped up on her face and hands to hear him. "I hate strawberries," she grumbled angrily.

"Maybe we can wave the magic mace over her," Lucas suggested. "It has the power to heal folks who are injured."

"Did you forget that it only works on people who are on the side of goodness?" Dribble asked him. "She's not exactly . . ."

Cap'n Bobbie glared at him. "I'm not exactly *what*?" she demanded.

"Um . . . it just won't work," Dribble mumbled. "Not this time."

Cap'n Bobbie looked down at the glob of half-chewed sandwich on the floor. "New kid. Mop that up!"

Lucas leaped to attention, grabbing a wet mop from the corner of the galley and swishing it around the floor.

"Get every bit of strawberry," the captain ordered as she scratched at the welts on her hands.

"Aye, aye, Cap'n," Lucas replied.

"I'm going up on deck," the captain continued. "I spotted that island this morning. The sunken treasure is almost mine!"

As the captain stomped out of the galley,

she told her crew, "If *I'm* done eating, yer *all* done—"

WHOMP!

Before the captain could bark out the rest of her order, she slipped on the wet floor.

"Ow! Me keister!" Cap'n Bobbie rubbed her bruised rear end. "Ye did that on purpose," she accused Lucas.

"I didn't, honest," Lucas assured her.

Cap'n Bobbie glowered at Lucas and Dribble. "I've had it with ye two. I don't want ye on me crew anymore. Yer gettin' off this ship."

Princess Pulverizer was amazed. Here she'd been trying to come up with a great plan to escape *The Seasick Soaker*, and all it took for Lucas and Dribble was a bit of strawberry jam and mop water.

Easy peasy.

Not.

"Yer walkin' the plank today," the captain continued.

Princess Pulverizer couldn't believe her ears. Had Cap'n Bobbie just said . . .

"That's right," Cap'n Bobbie continued. "It's straight down to Davy Jones's locker for you two!"

CHapter 7

"This is not going to end well," Lucas said with a frown as he looked at Princess Pulverizer and Dribble.

His voice sounded remarkably brave, all things considered. Princess Pulverizer was amazed at the power of the lion charm.

But Dribble didn't have a charm to help him be brave. "Okay, Princess Pulverizer, what's the plan?" he asked nervously.

"Plan?" the princess repeated.

"Don't you always have a plan?" the dragon asked.

"Usually," she agreed glumly. "But this . . ."

At just that moment, Cap'n Bobbie strode onto the deck. Unlike the princess and her friends, she was in a jolly mood. Parry the parrot was perched on her shoulder.

"Yo-ho-ho, me hearties!" Cap'n Bobbie greeted her crew. "What a day. First I spot that island with the sunken treasure. Now

I'm sending two prisoners into shark-infested waters." She rubbed her hands together gleefully. "I do love a good plank-walkin'."

"*Rawk.* Walk the plank," Parry added.

"*Argh!* Let's get this over with," Cap'n Bobbie announced. "Prisoners, to the plank with ye."

Princess Pulverizer's heart began to race. She had to do something, quickly.

"No!" she shouted. The word was out of her mouth before she could stop it.

Everyone on the ship stared at her.

"What did you say?" The captain angrily raised her argument-ender.

The sword glimmered in the sunlight. Suddenly, Princess Pulverizer had an idea.

"I challenge you to a duel!" she exclaimed.

Cap'n Bobbie started laughing. "Good joke."

"I'm not joking." Princess Pulverizer's heart was really pounding now. But she stood her ground, remembering what her father's knights always said—*never let your enemies see you sweat.*

"What's she doing?" Lucas whispered to Dribble.

Dribble shook his head. "I don't know," he admitted.

The princess knew *exactly* what she was doing. Or at least she hoped she did. "I challenge you to a duel," she insisted. "If I win, you let my friends go free. If you win, we all walk the plank."

"She's finally cracked," Dribble said.

The captain agreed. "Yer out of yer mind. I've made mincemeat out of much more skilled swordswomen than ye. Yer a nobody."

How insulting!

"I'm not a nobody!" Princess Pulverizer shouted back. "I've beaten my share of enemies, too!"

"I take it back," Cap'n Bobbie replied.

Princess Pulverizer smiled.

"Yer a *foolish* nobody!" the captain corrected herself. "And yer about to see what happens to anyone who challenges Cap'n Bobbie!"

Princess Pulverizer bit her lip nervously. Cap'n Bobbie could be possibly the meanest, most dangerous foe she'd ever faced. And that was saying something, considering she'd already defeated a giant monster made entirely of stinky cheese, an army of giant underground moles, and an overgrown hairy ogre.

But this was a gamble she had to take. Somebody had to defeat Cap'n Bobbie. And of all of them, Princess Pulverizer was the best one to do it.

That wasn't bragging. It was just a fact.

Lucas had learned how to duel in Knight School, but he hadn't been very successful. Not to mention that he was smaller than Princess Pulverizer, with short stubby legs. That put him at a disadvantage when it came to taking quick strides in a duel.

Dribble was bigger than either of them. He could *seem* scary—especially when he opened his huge snout and flared his wings out to the sides. Those wings seemed to be getting bigger every day! But there was a difference between seeming scary and being able to single-handedly win a battle against a stronger enemy.

That left only Princess Pulverizer.

"Argh!" Cap'n Bobbie exclaimed, slicing the air rapidly with her argument-ender. "Let's get this going."

Gulp. Cap'n Bobbie obviously knew her way around a blade. And Princess Pulverizer had never had a single fencing lesson. So, just in case she didn't win, the princess had already cooked up a plan.

She walked over to where Lucas and Dribble were standing.

"Where are ye goin'?" Cap'n Bobbie demanded.

"I'm having a word with my seconds," Princess Pulverizer told her.

"Oh, they're gonna be seconds." Cap'n Bobbie laughed. "And thirds. The sharks are always hungry."

Princess Pulverizer frowned. She hadn't meant that kind of seconds. She'd meant the seconds who made sure a sword fight was being fought fairly. "I need them to fetch my sword from the locker."

"All right," Cap'n Bobbie agreed. "But tell them to make it quick."

"Don't just get the sword," the princess whispered to her pals. "Get the other weapons as well. We may need them."

"But won't Cap'n Bobbie get suspicious if we come back on deck with everything we brought aboard?" Dribble asked.

"I don't think she'll notice," Princess Pulverizer said. "Look at her. All she's thinking about is the duel. She'll be too focused on me to see anything else."

It was true. Cap'n Bobbie was busy swishing her gleaming sword in the air. She was very focused on the deed at hand.

"While I keep her busy fighting, and the pirates are all watching us, you two need to get off this ship," Princess Pulverizer continued.

"How do we do that?" Lucas asked her.

"We're really close to that island now," she told him. "You can swim it."

"B-b-but what about the sharks?" Lucas stammered.

"They're all on the other side of the boat near the plank," Princess Pulverizer said. "The pirates have been feeding them fish to keep them there, waiting for you."

Dribble frowned. "Did you have to say that?"

"That means there won't be any sharks on the other side of the ship," the princess continued firmly. "You're going to jump off the side of the ship near the shore, where Meri is tied up. Free her and then ask her to lead the sharks away. I've never heard of sharks eating mermaids. I'm sure she will know how to deal with them."

Dribble nodded slowly. "It could work."

"I don't know. I'm a terrible swimmer," Lucas reminded her.

"No, you're not," Princess Pulverizer said encouragingly. "You just used to be afraid of the water. But you have that lion pendant now. You're braver."

"True," Lucas agreed, although he didn't sound completely convinced.

"What about you?" Dribble asked. "Cap'n Bobbie is going to be furious when she sees we're gone."

"Let's just hope I win this duel and she would have had to let us all go anyway." The princess looked solemnly at her friends. "It's the only way. We have to free Meri."

Dribble and Lucas nodded.

"Are they fetchin' yer sword or not?"

Cap'n Bobbie demanded.

"Go!" Princess Pulverizer ordered Dribble and Lucas.

"And hurry," Cap'n Bobbie added. "I'm losin' me patience."

◆ ◆ ◆ ◆ ◆

"Enough stalling!" Cap'n Bobbie shouted a few minutes later, when Dribble and Lucas arrived back on deck. Just as the princess had predicted, the captain was too busy preparing for the duel to notice what else Dribble and Lucas had brought with them.

Cap'n Bobbie held her sword high in the air. "En garde!"

"Wish me luck!" Princess Pulverizer called to her friends as she held out her sword and poised to advance on Cap'n Bobbie.

Just as the magic mirror had predicted.

The captain thrust her sword at Princess Pulverizer's chest. But the princess was quick. She blocked the sword with a perfect parry.

Princess Pulverizer advanced toward Cap'n Bobbie. The captain ducked out of the way in one smooth motion.

Click. Clack. Click. Clack.

The sound of swords blocked out everything else. Princess Pulverizer hoped Dribble and Lucas were making their escape. But she didn't dare take her eyes off Cap'n Bobbie for even an instant.

"Argh!" Cap'n Bobbie shouted as she lunged again.

The sword narrowly missed Princess Pulverizer's side as she stepped back in retreat.

The princess recovered quickly and stabbed right at the captain's neck.

Cap'n Bobbie was quick. She blocked the princess's sword and held it still in a skilled *prise de fer*.

Click. Clack. Click. Clack.

Cap'n Bobbie was certainly an expert swordswoman. But Princess Pulverizer was more than holding her own. It was even possible that she could . . .

"CAP'N!"

Princess Pulverizer's thoughts were interrupted by Stinky Stanley's shouts.

"Two of the prisoners are escapin'!"

Cap'n Bobbie immediately began barking out orders. "Tie this one up!" she ordered Stinky Stanley and Wiggle-Butt Willy. "The rest of you go grab the other two."

Before Princess Pulverizer could fight back, Stanley and Willy had grabbed her and were busy tying her arms at her sides.

As the princess struggled to free herself, Cap'n Bobbie glared angrily at her. "Ye made a very bad error," she growled. "And ye will pay. *Dearly*."

"They're gone, Cap'n," Stinky Stanley reported back a few moments later. "And they've taken that mermaid with 'em."

Wow! Princess Pulverizer had done it. She'd rescued Meri and saved her friends from a terrible fate. It was her most knightly deed of all.

"Ye have been trouble since I brought ye on this ship," Cap'n Bobbie told Princess Pulverizer. "But I know how to get rid of trouble. It's off the plank with ye! NOW!"

Princess Pulverizer had known that was coming. But hearing it come out of Cap'n Bobbie's mouth hit her hard. This was how her Quest of Kindness would end.

She would never see her father again.

She would never see Lucas and Dribble again.

And she would never become a knight.

The sadness was overwhelming. But surprisingly, Princess Pulverizer didn't regret going on the Quest of Kindness. She was proud to have helped so many folks along the way.

Her quest would be legendary. People would be talking about it for years.

Too bad she wouldn't be around to hear them.

◆ ◆ ◆ ◆ ◆

"*Argh!* Can't ye walk a little faster?" Cap'n Bobbie demanded as Willy and Tommy pushed the princess to the edge of the plank. "I have treasure to get to. And those sharks are hungry."

Princess Pulverizer bit her lip. She was determined not to show Cap'n Bobbie how scared she was. She would never give her the satisfaction. But it wasn't easy. Walking with her arms tied to her sides was painful. And while she still had her sword clutched in her hand, it was frustrating to be unable to use it.

"Enough of this!" Cap'n Bobbie growled. And with one hard shove, she pushed Princess Pulverizer off the plank to her doom.

chapter 8

Princess Pulverizer felt herself falling.
    This was it. The end. Any second now
she would hit the water and . . .

Boom. Princess Pulverizer landed.
But there was no splash.
No salt water in her eyes.
No sharks swimming toward her.
Because Princess Pulverizer hadn't landed in the water! She'd landed on Dribble's back.
In midair.

Dribble was flying! His grown-up wings had come in!

"Am I glad to see you!" Princess Pulverizer exclaimed. "I can't believe you're flying!"

"Me either," Dribble admitted. "I didn't know I could. It just happened. We freed Meri, my wings started flapping with joy, and the next thing I knew, I was in the air."

"It's just lucky he's strong enough to fly with us on his back," Lucas added.

"Not to mention both of your knapsacks, the mace, and the magic arrow," Dribble said. "You sure travel with a lot of stuff."

"We've been given a lot of tokens of gratitude on the Quest of Kindness," the princess reminded him. Then she added, "I bet Meri was glad to see you two."

"Lucas untied her net with his bare hands!" Dribble told her proudly.

"It was no big deal," Lucas said. "I should untie you, too," he added as he began undoing the knots that held Princess Pulverizer's arms to her sides.

"It was a *very* big deal," Dribble insisted. "You never saw anyone swim away so fast. Tired as she was, Meri knew she had to get away from the ship."

"And you were right—the sharks stayed away from us once Meri ordered them to," Lucas added. "You should have heard her yelling at them. I can't even repeat the words she used. Meri's one tough mermaid."

"But she did stop to say thank you. And give us this." Dribble held up Meri's beautiful pearl-covered comb.

"We've decided you should have it," Lucas told her.

"Why me?" she asked. "You're the one who freed her."

"But you're the one who most needs the comb's magic power," Dribble explained. "Meri said that whoever wears it will sing with a voice as lovely as a mermaid's."

"And your voice is . . . well . . . it's kinda . . ." Lucas struggled to find the right word.

"I get it." Princess Pulverizer took the comb from Lucas and put it in her hair. She began to sing. "*Laaaaaa!*"

Wow! Princess Pulverizer sounded just like a mermaid singing. In fact, she sounded so much like a mermaid, the pirates on *The Seasick Soaker* got very excited.

"I hear that mermaid!" one called out.

"Capture her!" Cap'n Bobbie demanded. "We need to know exactly where that treasure is."

Princess Pulverizer thought for a minute. "I don't know how far Meri has gotten," she said. "But I think we need to give her more of a head start before Cap'n Bobbie goes looking for her. Do you mind if we stay up here a little while longer? Are you strong enough, Dribble?"

"I think so," he replied. "What do you have in mind?"

Instead of answering, Princess Pulverizer began to sing, loud enough for the pirates to hear.

"The treasure's not underwater.
It's buried in the sand.
So instead of swimmin' you oughta
go find it on land."

Just as she expected, Cap'n Bobbie was

very interested in Princess Pulverizer's song. Especially because she thought *Meri* was singing.

"Rowers, get movin'. Bring the ship to shore!" she shouted. "Lower the gangplank. Onto land with all of ye. And bring shovels!"

A few minutes later, *The Seasick Soaker* was anchored just off the shore of the island. The pirates hurried down the gangplank with shovels in tow.

"Where should we start diggin', Cap'n?" Pete asked.

Princess Pulverizer started to sing again.

"You'll find the gems beneath the tree
with bright green stems
and coconuts three."

The pirates began searching for a tree with three coconuts on it. When they found it, they began to dig.

Princess Pulverizer let the sand fly for a bit. Then she began to sing again.

"Oops. My mistake.
The jewels are toward the island's tip,
not far from where you've anchored ship."

"Ye heard the mermaid!" Cap'n Bobbie shouted.

The pirates started running.

After a few minutes, Princess Pulverizer changed her tune again.

"No. It's not there, I fear.
Rather it's buried near the island's rear.
Look for a plant with flowers yellow,
and you'll find the gems, you lucky fellows."

"Get searching for that plant!" Cap'n

Bobbie ordered her men.

"This should keep them busy," Princess Pulverizer said. "Meri will be miles away before they realize there's no treasure."

"That's gonna be one tired crew," Lucas added as he studied all the holes being dug in the tiny island below.

"They're not the only ones getting tired," Dribble grumbled. "Flying's hard work."

"Then it's time to head to Empiria," Princess Pulverizer said.

"Yes!" Lucas agreed. "So you can go to Knight School."

"I don't know." Princess Pulverizer looked sadly down at the sea below. "Father might change his mind."

"You won't know until you ask him," Lucas said.

"Do either of you know which way to go?" Dribble wondered.

"I don't," Lucas admitted.

"Me either," Princess Pulverizer said. "But I do know who we can ask for directions."

Lucas looked around. "Who? It's just us and the clouds up here."

Princess Pulverizer grabbed the long arrow resting near her. "Remember what the mayor of Ire-Mire-Briar-Shire told us about this magic arrow? 'If ever the holder of the arrow finds themselves lost, it will always point them toward home.'"

The princess held the arrow in her hand. It twisted quickly to the left. "That way," the princess told her friends.

"Okay," Dribble said, flapping his wings harder. "Next stop, Empiria!"

Princess Pulverizer bit her lip nervously as they flew off. She was glad to be heading home. She only wished she knew what fate awaited her when she got there.

CHAPTER 9

"FATHER!"

Princess Pulverizer knew she was supposed to wait for King Alexander to speak before she said anything. And she knew she wasn't supposed to run into the king's throne room unannounced.

Those were the rules.

But the princess couldn't help herself. She was excited to see her father again. And hey, at least she'd cleaned herself up before she'd entered the room.

"Princess Ser . . . ," the king began
as he hugged her tight. But one look at
the expression on his daughter's face
stopped him short. "Princess Pulverizer,"
he corrected himself. "I am so glad to see
you have returned safe and sound."

"Me too," Princess Pulverizer replied.

"You've brought along a friend . . . and a *dragon*?" King Alexander sounded surprised at the sight of Dribble.

"Yes, but he's a kind dragon," Princess Pulverizer assured her father. "And brave, too. He and Lucas saved me more than once on my Quest of Kindness."

"Well then, you are both welcome in my palace. With gratitude," the king added.

Dribble and Lucas both bowed deeply.

"We shall have a banquet to celebrate your safe return!" King Alexander announced. "I'll tell the chef . . ."

"Oh, there's no need for that," Princess Pulverizer interrupted her father. "Dribble is a better chef than anyone in the whole palace." She turned to her friend. "Go ahead, show him."

Dribble looked a little unsure. But the princess gave him an encouraging smile, then pulled a loaf of bread and a pound of pungent provolone cheese from her sack.

Dribble made a sandwich, held it near his snout, and let out a flame—not too high and not too low. Just perfect for grilling.

"Oh my!" King Alexander exclaimed. "That's quite a fire you've got going."

Princess Pulverizer tried hard not to giggle. It was rare that her father seemed nervous around anyone or anything. But it was clear that a fire-breathing dragon in the middle of his throne room was having just that effect.

"Here, your highness," Dribble said, handing the king a perfectly grilled cheese sandwich on a plate.

King Alexander took the sandwich
from the dragon and stared at it.

"Go ahead, Father," Princess Pulverizer
said. "Take a bite."

"I think I'm going to need a napkin," the king said.

"Just use your sleeve," Princess Pulverizer told him. "I always do."

King Alexander laughed and took a bite of the sandwich. "My goodness!" he exclaimed. "This is scrumptious."

Dribble smiled proudly as the king hungrily devoured the delicious sandwich.

Princess Pulverizer took a deep breath. Now that her father had a full stomach and was in a good mood, the time was right to ask him for permission to go to Knight School.

"Father, I have managed to do what you asked," Princess Pulverizer said. "Together with Lucas and Dribble, we have completed eight good deeds. And we have the tokens of gratitude to prove it."

One by one, the princess laid out the gifts she and her friends had gathered on their quest.

There was the ruby ring given to them by the Queen of Shmergermeister as a thank-you for finding stolen jewels, and the sword the King of Salamistonia presented them with for bringing laughter back to his kingdom.

There was also the arrow the mayor of Ire-Mire-Briar-Shire had given them for returning all the cows, sheep, and goats to his village, and the giant mace that had been a gift from the King of Yabko-kokomo, to thank the princess and her friends for returning his kidnapped subjects.

The princess showed her father the

lovely hand mirror given to her by the good witch of Starats. Then she nodded toward Dribble, who proudly laid his magic handkerchief beside the mirror. It had been a gift from the mayor of Beeten Wheeten for their help in cleaning up the village's polluted water.

Finally the princess placed the comb that Meri had given them beside the handkerchief. Then she stood back and waited for her father's praise.

The king looked at the table. "I only count seven," he told Princess Pulverizer.

"I have the eighth one," Lucas said. "It's here around my neck." He showed the king the lion pendant King Harvey had presented to him after the trio had found a way to keep him safe from being poisoned by enemies.

"He never takes it off," Princess Pulverizer explained. "It has a magic power that brings him bravery when he needs it."

"I will take it off if you want me to," Lucas told the princess. "Anything to help."

"There's no need," King Alexander assured him. "I can see that you three have most definitely helped a great number of people." He smiled fondly at Princess Pulverizer. "I am proud of you, my daughter. You have done exactly as I instructed."

Well . . . not *exactly*.

The princess thought for a moment. Maybe she could get away with not telling her father about having broken his rules when *The Seasick Soaker* floated out to sea. He didn't have to know *everything* about the Quest of Kindness, did he?

Yes. He probably did. Because not telling him was pretty much like lying. And lying wasn't knightly at all.

"I didn't *completely* follow your instructions, Father," Princess Pulverizer admitted slowly. "For the most part I did. But there was this one adventure, when we were on a pirate ship, and we . . . well . . . we kind of sailed out to sea."

"Kind of?" the king repeated, sounding displeased. "How does one *kind of* sail out to sea?"

"Okay, we did sail out to sea," the princess continued. "But I couldn't . . ."

"You were only supposed to go as far as the ocean," King Alexander said, interrupting her. "Not *into* the ocean."

"I know," Princess Pulverizer agreed. "But a mermaid was in danger. And I had to help her. The only way I could save her—and my friends—was by staying aboard the ship and seeing the job through."

"It's true, your highness," Lucas added. "She put her own life in danger to save all of us."

Princess Pulverizer smiled gratefully at her friend. She knew how much bravery it took for him to stand up to a king. The old Lucas would have been cowering in the corner and stammering nervously in his presence. But not anymore.

Unfortunately, it didn't seem to matter to her father. King Alexander shook his head disappointedly. "I don't like having my orders disobeyed," he told Princess

Pulverizer. "I don't like it at all. I'll have to think about this."

Princess Pulverizer gulped. For as long as she'd been on the Quest of Kindness, she'd dreamed of coming back to Empiria, telling her father about all the good deeds she'd done, and having him grant her wish of going to Knight School.

It was all she wanted.

It was all she'd *ever* wanted.

Now she wasn't so sure it was going to happen. She looked up at her father, scanning his face for some sign of what decision he might make.

But the king was giving Princess Pulverizer no clue as to what her future held.

CHAPTER 10

"Princess Pulverizer!" Sir Irontrousers shouted. "Come down from there right now! Knights-in-training do not hang from the ceiling—unless they are surprising an enemy from above."

Princess Pulverizer frowned. She really didn't want to come down. It was so much fun swinging from the rafters, high above the other knights-in-training. But she also knew that Sir Irontrousers was her teacher. And that meant that he was in charge.

Still, another swing or two couldn't hurt . . .

So she swung. Back and forth.

Back and forth.

Back and . . .

"WHOA!" The princess let out a loud yelp as she lost her grip on the rafter.

CLANK. Her new armor made a loud noise as she landed.

SPLASH! The princess's royal bottom landed right in a big bowl of ooey-gooey purple pomegranate pudding.

SMASH. Spoons, forks, knives, teacups, and saucers careened to the floor. There was broken china everywhere.

All the other knights-in-training went scrambling away from the table.

Princess Pulverizer looked up at Sir Irontrousers and waited for him to yell at her—just the way Lady Frump at the Royal School of Ladylike Manners had.

But he didn't. Instead, her new teacher said, "What an excellent way to cause confusion. That will be very helpful to you in battle."

Princess Pulverizer smiled. She was so happy to be in Knight School, where her talents could be appreciated and even encouraged. Thank goodness her father had understood why she had needed to disobey him, and had given his permission for her to attend.

"However," Sir Irontrousers continued, "we are *not* in the middle of a battle right now. We are in a dining hall. You have just ruined the dessert that Dribble, our chef, has prepared for us."

Princess Pulverizer looked up from the pomegranate pudding and flashed her friend an apologetic grin. "I'm sorry, Dribble," she said. "I'm sure the pudding was delicious."

"It was!" Lucas said. He was sitting at the far end of the table, surrounded by a group of boys. "One of his best yet."

"You tell her, Brave Buccaneer!" one of the other boys cheered him.

Princess Pulverizer smiled. No one would be laughing Lucas out of Knight School this time around.

Dribble was happy, too. His dream of being a real chef had come true. Everyone in Knight School loved the meals he prepared for them. King Alexander had done a good deed when he'd given him the job.

But neither Dribble nor Lucas was as happy to be at Knight School as Princess Pulverizer. And best of all, she'd *earned* the right to be here.

"You're going to have to clean up this mess," Sir Irontrousers told her.

"Yes sir," Princess Pulverizer replied. "Right away." She dipped her finger into a pool of pomegranate pudding and tasted it. "This *is* delicious," she told Dribble.

"*Was* delicious," Dribble corrected her. "It looks like there won't be any seconds today." But he didn't sound angry. The dragon was used to Princess Pulverizer's antics by that point.

As she cleaned up the mess, Princess

Pulverizer glanced out the window. Across the way, she spotted a row of young girls in the palace ballroom. Lady Frump was teaching them how to dance.

Tap. Tap. Hop. The girls were moving in a perfect line—all except the smallest of them. She was staring intently out the window, looking longingly at the group of knights-in-training in the courtyard below.

The littlest girl looked up and spotted Princess Pulverizer watching her. Her face scrunched up with embarrassment.

But there was no need. Princess Pulverizer understood completely. She gave the littlest girl a big grin.

The littlest girl smiled back shyly.

Princess Pulverizer shot her an encouraging wink and went back to cleaning. She was anxious to mop up all the purple pomegranate pudding as quickly as possible.

After all, Princess Pulverizer had her own lessons to learn.

Here.

In Knight School.

Where she'd always belonged.

author & illustrator

nancy krulik

is the author of more than two
hundred books for children and
young adults, including three
New York Times Best Sellers.
She is the creator of several successful book
series for children, including Katie Kazoo,
Switcheroo; How I Survived Middle School;
George Brown, Class Clown; and Magic Bone.
Visit Nancy at realnancykrulik.com.

ian mcginty

is an animation director, voice
actor, and comic book artist/
writer based in Los Angeles,
California. He has worked for
Nickelodeon Studios, Marvel, BOOM! Studios,
Oni Press, and many more. Check out Ian's
work at ianmcginty.com.